WISDOM Wagon
Devotions for Children

Be Prepared

A Lesson in Being a Wise Student

(Based on the parable of the Girls and the Oil)

Hope McCardy and **Lisa Bastian**
with BROOKE & LEE
Illustrated by Brea Coyoca

BE PREPARED

Copyright © 2021 by Hope McCardy, Lisa Bastian and Color Me Reading Publishers.

All rights reserved. No part of this book may be reproduced, stored in a retrieval system, or used in any manner whatsoever without permission in writing from the authors. The only exception is brief quotations in printed reviews.

Scriptures quoted from the International Children's Bible®, copyright ©1986, 1988, 1999, 2015 by Tommy Nelson. Used by permission.

For information, please email us or visit our websites:

www.brookeandlee.com
info@brookeandlee.com

www.empoweringyourhope.com
info@empoweringyourhope.com

Color Me Reading Books – YouTube page

ISBN: 978-0-9976331-8-4

Printed in the United States of America.

Precious Child,

We want to share with you that you are special. You were made *in an amazing and wonderful way* (Psalm 139:14). In fact, *God has made us what we are* (Ephesians 2:10). And you, dear child, are His greatest creation.

According to Jeremiah 29:11, God has a plan for your life – a very good plan! He wants to bless you and give you a future full of hope.

Because you are a Boy or Girl of Purpose, we want to encourage you to be WISE. We wish to inspire you to choose to walk in WISDOM every day. It is our deep desire that you learn to do your best in whatever is placed before you.

Hence, as you go through Jesus' parable, *The Girls and the Oil,* which is adapted and shared in this book, please listen carefully with your heart. In addition, as you complete all of the various activities, our prayer is that you truly understand how important preparation is in learning how to be a Good Student.

So,

Get on the WISDOM Wagon and BE PREPARED!

Contents

BE PREPARED: Part 1 1

  Five Wise Friends 3

      ▪ WISDOM Wagon Activities 7

BE PREPARED: Part 2 13

  Five Unwise Pals 15

      ▪ WISDOM Wagon Activities 19

BE PREPARED: Part 3 24

  End of Year Examinations 26

      ▪ WISDOM Wagon Activities 31

BE PREPARED: Part 4 37

  Being Prepared Pays Off 39

      ▪ WISDOM Wagon Activities 43

Be Prepared Song 48

Other COLOR ME Reading Titles Available 53

Be Prepared Formula:

Reading Content: 100%

Coloring Content: 17%

Activity Content: 12%

Symbols Used

 Lamp filled with oil: represents being **wise** or WISDOM

 Lamp with little oil: represents being **unwise**

A little bit to color,
A little more to read.
A little bit of courage,
As we aim to plant a seed.

Through colors and writing,
Through moments we share.
To be creative and inviting,
For children everywhere.

Learning we expect,
But fun we require.
The only rule we accept,
Is to *believe, imagine, and inspire.*

Let's Get on the WISDOM Wagon, Kids!

Where...

W is for **WISE**
I is for **INSIGHTFUL**
S is for **SENSITIVE**
D is for **DISCERNING**
O is for **OBEDIENT**
M is for **MOTIVATED**

Be Wise and Choose WISDOM Every Day!

BE PREPARED

Part 1

Five Wise Friends

Matthew 25:1-5

"At that time the kingdom of heaven will be like ten girls who went to wait for the bridegroom. They took their lamps with them. Five of the girls were foolish and five were wise. The five foolish girls took their lamps, but they did not take more oil for the lamps to burn. The wise girls took their lamps and more oil in jars. The bridegroom was very late. All the girls became sleepy and went to sleep."

WISDOM Wagon Bible Verse

But if any of you needs wisdom, you should ask God for it. God is generous. He enjoys giving to all people, so God will give you wisdom.

James 1:5

Five Wise Friends

There once were five friends who did everything together at their primary school; they ate lunch together and did their homework together. At PE time, they tried hard to be on the same team even.

One special thing they held in common was being members of their school's *Helping Hands Club*. This club that met on Wednesdays at lunchtime was a highlight for the buddies and created a stronger bond for their friendship. At the *Helping Hands Club*, the friends were given opportunities to raise money for the poor in the community by helping with different fund-raising events.

On one weekend, each month, they would join in with the *Helping Hands Clubs* from other schools. The friends and their leaders faithfully delivered food packages and toiletry items to homeless people. Meeting people that are poor and in great need caused the buddies to be grateful for what they have. It also pushed them to work harder in school to prepare themselves for a better future. These playmates encouraged one another to do and to be their very best at all times.

WISDOM Wagon Prayer

Dear Lord, I need Your wisdom. Please help me to be wise like the five wise friends in the story and push me to work hard in school. Inspire me to also give a helping hand to those in need. In Jesus' name. Amen.

WISDOM Wagon Activities

Wise Advice: What does our Bible verse say to do if you need wisdom?

_____
_____
_____
_____
_____

Make a List: Give five (5) ways you can offer a helping hand to others.

a. _____
b. _____
c. _____
d. _____
e. _____

Think About it: How should you go about choosing your good friends?

_____
_____
_____
_____
_____

Fun Time Activity

Ask God for WISDOM!

(James 1:5)

Fun Time Activity

Ask God for WISDOM!

(James 1:5)

Your Special Page

On this page, you can draw, record your thoughts, or anything else you would like to do. Have fun!

BE PREPARED
Part 2

Five Unwise Pals

Matthew 25:1-5

"At that time the kingdom of heaven will be like ten girls who went to wait for the bridegroom. They took their lamps with them. Five of the girls were foolish and five were wise. The five foolish girls took their lamps, but they did not take more oil for the lamps to burn. The wise girls took their lamps and more oil in jars. The bridegroom was very late. All the girls became sleepy and went to sleep."

WISDOM Wagon Bible Verse

Stop your foolish ways, and you will live.
Be a person of understanding.

Proverbs 9:6

At the same school, five other young pals enjoyed one another's company and created a close bond by taking delight in gossiping about other students.

They often tricked other school children into cheating and sharing answers with them when they didn't care enough to do their own homework.

These pals spent their break times talking about the latest YouTube fad, other kid shows on TV, and what games they enjoyed playing. They had no interest in doing any schoolwork and encouraged each other to find the latest game on their cell phones. Also, one of their favorite pastimes was to play tricks on their classmates.

As a group, they were more interested in recess than in doing their lessons.

WISDOM Wagon Prayer

Dear Lord, I need Your wisdom. Help me not to be foolish like the five unwise pals in the story. Please teach me how to be a person of understanding. In Jesus' name. Amen.

WISDOM Wagon Activities

Wise Advice: What does our Bible verse encourage you to do?

_____
_____
_____
_____

Unscramble: Unscramble these words that may describe the unwise actions of the five (5) pals.

1. PGOSIS
   _____

2. CKISTTERR
   _____

3. EATCHING
   _____

4. CREFRAEE
   _____

5. ZALY
   _____

6. LEID
   _____

Think About it: Do you relate to these five (5) pals? If so, what changes will you make today?

_____
_____
_____
_____

Answers: (1) gossip, (2) trickster, (3) cheating, (4) carefree, (5) lazy, (6) idle

Fun Time Activity

Be a Person of Understanding!

(Proverbs 9:6)

Fun Time Activity

Be a Person of Understanding!

(Proverbs 9:6)

BE PREPARED
Part 3

End of Year Examinations

Matthew 25:6-10

"At midnight someone cried out, 'The bridegroom is coming! Come and meet him!' Then all the girls woke up and got their lamps ready. But the foolish girls said to the wise, 'Give us some of your oil. Our lamps are going out.' The wise girls answered, 'No. The oil we have might not be enough for all of us. Go to the people who sell oil and buy some for yourselves.'

So the five foolish girls went to buy oil. While they were gone, the bridegroom came. The girls who were ready went in with the bridegroom to the wedding feast. Then the door was closed and locked."

WISDOM Wagon Bible Verse

So be very careful how you live. Do not live like those who are not wise. Live wisely. I mean that you should use every chance you have for doing good....

Ephesians 5:15-16

The time came for the closing examinations of the school year. This testing was crucial for the students as it would determine who would be able to move up to the next grade level.

The group of friends in the Helping Hands Club had followed a consistent study schedule throughout the school year – as well as they completed and turned in all their homework assignments. These buddies got to their beds early the night before the exams, ate breakfast before going to school, and they each brought their writing instruments, which made them well equipped for taking the tests.

As for the group of gossip pals, when they realized that they had not put in any time studying and had neglected to listen in class or do much homework, they started to panic. Their panic turned to angry accusations and harsh blaming of each other. They said mean things to one another until one of them spoke loudly and suggested, "Wait a minute, we should just ask that group of friends over there." [She pointed to the buddies from the *Helping Hands Club*], "Maybe they can give us a quick study session this half-hour before the exams begin."

The gossip pals approached the *Helping Hands* friends and asked them to help them with a quick review of their classwork. The *Helping Hands* group felt really sorry for the gossip pals but explained that they could not help because they had to use this time before the exam to be quiet and review their own work themselves.

WISDOM Wagon Prayer

Dear Lord, I don't want to get to the end of the school year as the unwise pals did. Push me to work hard all through the year and inspire me to take out enough time to prepare well for my exams. In Jesus' name. Amen.

WISDOM Wagon Activities

Wise Advice: When our Bible verse says to "live wisely," how does this inspire you to use your time? Explain.

_____

_____

_____

_____

_____

True (T) or False (F): Read the statement and write "T" or "F" in the space provided.

   a. It is wise to work hard and steady _____
   b. A child should never do his or her homework _____
   c. Talking bad about others is a good thing _____
   d. Cheating on tests is wrong _____
   e. To choose WISDOM is sensible _____

Think About it: What wise choices will you make right now?

1. _____
2. _____
3. _____

Answers: (a) T, (b) F, (c) F, (d) T, (e) T

Fun Time Activity

Choose God's WISDOM to Live Wisely!

(Ephesians 5:15)

Fun Time Activity

Choose God's WISDOM to Live Wisely!

(Ephesians 5:15)

Your Special Page

On this page, you can draw, record your thoughts,
or anything else you would like to do. Have fun!

BE PREPARED
Part 4

Being Prepared Pays Off

Matthew 25:11-13

"Later the others came back. They called, 'Sir, sir, open the door to let us in.' But the bridegroom answered, 'I tell you the truth, I don't know you.' So always be ready. You don't know the day or the time the Son of Man will come."

WISDOM Wagon Bible Verse

The wise person is rewarded by his wisdom. But a person who makes fun of wisdom will suffer for it.

Proverbs 9:12

Being Prepared Pays Off

The story did not end well for the five unprepared, unfocused gossip pals. Like the five girls in Jesus' parable who did not bring extra oil to refill their lamps and missed the Bridegroom, these pals realized that they began the school year with the same capabilities and potential to ace the exams as with the *Helping Hands friends*. Had they, like the *Helping Hands* buddies, paid attention in class, completed homework assignments, and taken the time to review their work, they would have been well prepared for the final examinations.

All five of the wise friends easily advanced to the next grade level.

As for the unwise pals, they are still anxiously waiting to see if they somehow squeezed through to the next grade.

41

WISDOM Wagon Prayer

Dear Lord, I pray that You would help me, every day, to choose to work hard to be prepared. May I be inspired and encouraged to live wisely. In Jesus' name. Amen.

WISDOM Wagon Activities

Wise Advice: Write out your WISDOM Wagon Bible Verse (Proverbs 9:12) and read it over and over again.

_____
_____
_____
_____
_____

For you to Compose: Write your own prayer asking God to make you wise.

_____
_____
_____
_____
_____

Think About it: How can you tell whether someone is wise or not?

_____
_____
_____
_____

Let's Get on the WISDOM Wagon and Stay on the WISDOM Wagon!

Fun Time Activity

44

A Wise Person is Rewarded by his WISDOM.

(Proverbs 9:12)

Fun Time Activity

A Wise Person is Rewarded by his WISDOM.

(Proverbs 9:12)

Be Prepared Song
Be Wise; Be Prepared

Wise children are quite prepared;
They fill their lamps with oil.
Wise kids are so very smart;
They plant seeds in good soil.

Wise children are quite prepared;
More oil for their lamps they bring.
Wise kids are so very bright;
They work hard to please our King.

Chorus
Boys, be wise and girls, be wise;
You have to decide to be wise.
Be prepared; be well prepared;
You have to decide to be prepared.

But,
Unwise kids are not prepared;
They leave their lamps to wane.
Unwise kids are not so smart;
They plant seed without gain.

Unwise kids are not prepared;
Spare lamp-oil they leave at home.
Unwise kids are not so sharp;
They allow their minds to roam.

Chorus

Boys, be wise and girls, be wise;
You have to decide to be wise.
Be prepared; be well prepared;
You have to decide to be prepared.

So,
Dear children, make up your mind;
Be studious and kind.
Kids, be sure to study hard;
So, you're not left behind.

Please, children, make up your mind;
Pay attention in your class.
Yes, kids, you be very smart;
To make sure your grade you pass.

Chorus

Boys, be wise and girls, be wise;
You have to decide to be wise.
Be prepared; be well prepared;
You have to decide to be prepared.

Boys, be wise and girls, be wise;
You have to decide to be wise.
Be prepared; be well prepared;
You have to decide, decide, decide…, to be prepared!
Be prepared! Be prepared! Be prepared! Be prepared.

Fun Time Activity

50

Be Wise; Be Prepared!

Be Prepared: Select to be a Wise Student by Choosing WISDOM Every Day!

Remember,

W is for **WISE**

I is for **INSIGHTFUL**

S is for **SENSITIVE**

D is for **DISCERNING**

O is for **OBEDIENT**

M is for **MOTIVATED**

Only the Lord gives wisdom. Knowledge and understanding come from him.

Proverbs 2:6

Check out some of our other books!

Color Me Reading

Younger Kids:

Dave the Brave

Mr. Friend

Crayons and Colors

Where Da Conch Gone

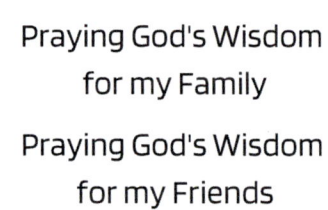

Older Kids:

Praying God's Wisdom for my Family

Praying God's Wisdom for my Friends

Praying God's Wisdom for Myself

Share, Save, Spend

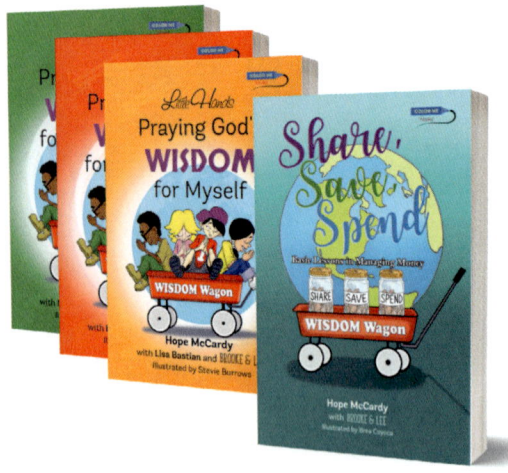

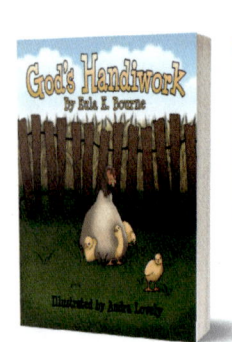

Recommended Books by Other Authors:

God's Handiwork
by: Eula E. Bourne

GB and the Coconut Tree
by: Gregory Burrows

Don't forget to go to our website.

Enjoy listening to the **songs** that go along with the books!

www.brookeandlee.com